MW01171794

SPICY SPRING FLING

Gwyn McNamee

Christy Anderson

Spicy Spring Fling

© 2022 Gwyn McNamee & Christy Anderson

BLURB

Bobby Sweet is a legend in the kitchen.
Rumor is, he really knows how to handle an eggplant.
It's the entire reason I'm here writing this article about him for the paper.
But I keep having to remind myself to stay professional.
Because things are *really* heating up in his kitchen.
And the rumors are true.
Bobby's eggplant is something to behold.
Large.
Thick.
Exactly what I've been craving.
It makes my mouth water...
Along with other parts of me...
The only question is, will I be able to handle all of it?
I can certainly try.
A spicy spring fling with the hot chef may be just what I need...

Chapter One

ASHLEY

"**O**h, my God...it's *huge!*" The words tumble from my mouth before I can stop them. Anyone looking at me right now would probably see my eyes bulging out of my head like some old school cartoon character. Because I've never seen anything like it. "*Far* bigger than any I've ever seen before, and I've seen a lot. Look, my hand can't close around it."

The tips of my fingers don't even touch...

How is this even possible?

It's not natural.

It's freaking HUGE!

My mouth waters simply thinking about what's coming from this thick specimen of absolute beauty and perfection.

"Stop molesting the vegetables!" The elderly man's screech interrupts my appreciation of the purple produce.

The eggplant tumbles from my grip and back into the wooden basket on Old Jerry's table as he scowls at me from behind his stand with condemnation. He crosses his arms over his chest, tapping his foot in reproach and glaring daggers that could slice open the toughest skin.

Shit.

Old Jerry is kind of scary.

And here I thought quaint towns like this were supposed to be full of friendly, laid-back locals. This certainly isn't one of them.

I hold up my hands, palms out, in apology and do my best to look contrite. "Sorry, I was just surprised at how *massive* it is."

A snicker beside me sends a warm rush through my body and makes me turn to my left, where sexy Chef Bobby Sweet has his hand over his mouth, barely containing a laugh at my expense.

Heat creeps up my neck and over my cheeks despite the light spring breeze flowing through the streets of Smalltownsville.

Shit.

Did I really say all that out loud?

That definitely sounded bad.

Bad. Bad. Bad. Super bad.

I'm supposed to be *interviewing* him for the newspaper article, not making lewd sexual innuendos at the damn farmer's market in front of an old man Bobby only *just* introduced me to minutes ago. I barely even know Bobby. It's only been thirty minutes since we met at the entrance of the market to shop and go through my questions for my story. And I've already made a total fool of myself going on and on about the ginormous faux-phallus.

Talk about cringeworthy.

Way to go, Ash.

Real professional.

Ashley Wells will *not* be winning a Pulitzer anytime soon, but maybe I can get into writing lady porn about big vegetables...

Bobby lowers his hand, a grin still tilting his perfect lips, and leans toward me slightly, so Old Jerry can't hear him. "To be fair, it *is* pretty big."

"That's what she said." The old, overused joke slips out before I can bite it back, like I'm goofing around with an old friend instead of someone I just met.

He waggles his dark eyebrows playfully, and I can't help but giggle in a completely unprofessional way, drawing an annoyed look from the purveyor of the stand who is apparently *not* amused by our jokes at his produce's expense.

Jokes we should *most definitely* not be making, given the circumstances.

This is an interview.

I'm doing my *job*.

Keep reminding yourself of that, Ash.

Bobby retreats from me slightly, then grabs the *aubergine* in question and squeezes it gently. "But that's exactly why I came to his stand today. He has the best and biggest produce in town. He has massive greenhouses where he overwinters his plants, so he has eggplants months before they're usually available. "

"I can see that." Scanning the table in front of us, everything practically glows in the bright mid-afternoon sunlight—perfect, like the type of stock photo our paper might use for the very article I'm writing. It looks better than anything we have available in the supermarkets back in Milwaukee. "Do you only buy from him?"

The subject of my interview offers a slight shrug of his broad shoulders and puts the eggplant and several more like it into the fabric bags in his left hand. Old Jerry observes him carefully, and Bobby grabs a twenty out of his wallet and drops it on the table, earning a nod of acknowledgement from the grumpy farmer.

"I also get some items from other people, but no one has anything as big or succulent as Old Jerry."

I fight another laugh and the desire to glance down at the perfect jeans encasing Bobby's "eggplant."

It's a battle I lose.

After my pre-interview research uncovered a comment from his ex-girlfriend on an article about his famous spicy moussaka...lamenting the loss of not only his cooking but also his massive...package, I can't get it out of my head.

I bet it's big and succulent, too...

That same sexual heat sizzles through my body, and I remove my jean jacket and drape it over my arm, hoping the breeze against my mostly exposed skin in the white sundress will cool off the crazy response every fiber of my being seems to have being around the award-winning chef.

The very thing I need whips down the streets and blows across me, chilling me slightly, enough that I regain my composure and follow Bobby to the next stall—absolutely *not* watching how amazing his ass looks in the perfectly fit denim—where he examines some heirloom tomatoes.

"Now tomatoes..."—he holds one up and squeezes it gently, but all that does is conjure images of those large hands and deft fingers digging into my skin —"Mrs. Beasley has the best tomatoes."

"Oh, really?" I clear my throat to dislodge the desire in it, raise an eyebrow, and glance over my shoulder at the stand we just departed. "Cheating on Old Jerry?"

Bobby grins. "No, even *he* buys his tomatoes from her. She does something to her soil." With a conspiratorial look around to ensure no one is in earshot, he leans in, monitoring the old woman watching us from her folding chair behind the table. His minty breath flutters over me, heating me again more than the overhead sun. "I think she puts her dog's shit in it as fertilizer."

That splashes a much-needed cold bucket of water on my libido.

"Ewww." I jerk my face back from his reflexively and make a very unladylike gagging sound. "Really?"

He chuckles, his chest vibrating against my shoulder. "What do you think fertilizer is? Just shit in one form or another."

"I guess...but still...ewww."

Sometimes, it's better *not* to think about how food is grown or where it comes from.

"Well, whatever she does"—he brings the tomato to his nose and lets his eyes drift closed as he inhales —"they are absolutely divine."

A little moan slips from his mouth and a zing of electricity straight between my legs—happily distracting me from thoughts of doggie fertilizer.

Suddenly, I'm feeling less grossed out and more...

Down girl.

This is a professional interview with Chef Bobby Sweet for the newspaper—not a date, not an opportunity to swoon over the man with the reputation for delicious food and a big...heart.

But God, it's hard not to with his striking amber eyes, quick smile, and dashing Disney-prince good looks. Not to mention a backside so perfect and firm that you could bounce a quarter off it.

Stop looking at the man's ass, Ash.

At least I'm not alone. Every woman out and about at the farmers' market today seems to take notice of him. It's no wonder Sweet Home Kitchen has been killing it since he returned from culinary school a few years ago and took over the family business.

Though, his famous spicy moussaka may have something to do with it, too.

Good looks *and* talent—the *complete package.*

Not to mention what he's packing in those jeans.

Some woman out there is damn *lucky.*

Bobby throws five huge heirloom tomatoes into his bag and tosses a twenty across the table to the old woman who must be Mrs. Beasley. She slowly rises from the chair to grab it, the small dog at her feet barking at her movement.

"She puts her dog's shit in it as fertilizer..."

All I can think about is what Bobby said, and I cringe and watch Mrs. Beasley snatch up the money while the tiny supplier of said fertilizer spins in circles.

I narrow my eyes on the bill in her hand. "Are you really buying twenty dollars' worth of everything?"

It certainly doesn't seem like it. A few dollars at each table, at most, but since we first met up, he's dropped at least a hundred bucks on various fresh ingredients, including farm-fresh lamb, herbs, home-made cheeses, and a variety of greenhouse-grown vegetables.

He playfully nudges me with his shoulder and grins. "Of course not, but it's a farmers' market, and it's the first of the season. They could really use the money this time of year. People in town always overpay. It's kind of what we do in Smalltownsville. You don't do that where you are from?"

The personal question makes goosebumps pebble across my skin, and I rub at the back of my neck as I debate whether I should answer him.

This is supposed to be an interview about *him* and his restaurant, not an opportunity for him to question me about my personal life. Yet, somehow, that's where we've ended up naturally. Conversation has flowed so easily between us this entire time, so much so that it would be the best first date I've ever been on—if this were *actually* a date.

Which it's NOT, Ash!

I dodge a running child and tuck a strand of hair that the light wind blew in my face back behind my ear. "Not really. Milwaukee's weird, though. There are farmers' markets and other things that can sometimes make it feel like a small town, but we mostly shop at supermarkets and eat a lot of takeout. At least, I do."

It almost feels like committing a cardinal sin admitting that to him, knowing how important using fresh and local ingredients is to him and his restaurant's style. He hasn't stopped talking about it since the moment we met up here—shopping local, getting the highest quality for the best price but being a loyal customer for the providers, putting time, love, and care into each and every dish.

Bobby snorts and shakes his head, as if the idea is both comical and upsetting. "I know what you mean. I spent a lot of time there."

"Really?" In all my research on the restaurant and Bobby Sweet, Milwaukee never came up. If he opened a place there, he would rake in big bucks he can't possibly make in a small town like this. "I don't remember seeing anything about Milwaukee in your background when I was preparing for this interview."

He nods slowly. "Sure did. I was helping a friend

from culinary school set up his restaurant there. Spent about six months assisting with creating the menu, choosing the décor for the interior, finding the right kitchen staff, and anything else he needed, but I haven't been back in a while."

"Because you're too busy here..."

That playful grin pulls at the corner of his lips again. "It's a good problem to have."

"I bet." And this is the perfect time to segue back to the task at hand and away from personal things that have no business in this interview. "To what do you contribute the restaurant's success? You coming back? To mixing things up?"

Bobby pauses in the middle of the street that's been closed down for the weekly weekend market and examines me while people stroll along past us. "You trying to get me to say something that will piss off my mom?"

"What?" It takes a minute for my brain to fully register his question and how it relates to what I just asked. "Oh, no! God, no! I hadn't even..." I press my hand against my face, embarrassment flaming my cheeks again. "That's not what I meant."

Wonderful. Insult the man's mother.

Sweet Home Kitchen has been in the Sweet family for three generations. His British grandparents opened it in 1952 and kept it running until they passed it on to their son and daughter-in-law, Bobby's mother, in the 70s, the woman I basically said cooks like shit.

"From what I hear, your mother's recipes have become legendary here. I just meant—"

"I know what you meant." He nudges my shoulder playfully again. "I was just giving you shit."

"Oh..." Relief floods my system, the tension releasing almost immediately, to be replaced by a tingling feeling where his body touched mine. The gentle breeze blows his cologne my way. I inhale, and my toes dang near curl in my shoes at a scent that is all man and uniquely all Bobby. Rich and crisp at the same time. "Good."

The last thing I need is for the subject of my article to clam up and decide he doesn't want to give me any information or answer any of my questions because he can't be confident in how I'll present him or his family's legacy.

"So, to answer your question, I brought back a few new techniques and ideas. That much is true. But at the heart of all my cooking are the things my mother and grandmother taught me." A wistful smile tilts his lips. "The old school way of preparing dishes and ensuring they're absolutely perfect."

Oh, my gosh.

He's so dang, well...sweet.

"Is that what you do with your famous spicy moussaka dish?"

It's the very reason I'm even interviewing him today. Sweet Home Kitchen was voted one of top five best restaurants in the Midwest, apparently because of the dish—the focus of today's profile, along with the man behind it.

His amber eyes take on a thoughtful, faraway look

for a moment, then he glances at me as we continue to stroll through the market. "That's an old family recipe from my Greek grandmother on my mother's side. I just put a little spin on it."

"Oh, that sounds interesting. What sort of spin?"

Bobby leans in, his lips brushing my ear in a way that is definitely too close for the professional interaction we're supposed to be having. "If I tell you that, I'd have to kill you."

Chapter Two

ASHLEY

"**K**ill me?" I recoil slightly and press my hand against my chest in mock horror, fighting a grin. "Who are you, James Bond?"

Bobby barks out a laugh that floats through the air and draws the attention of several people walking past us. We get a few awkward looks, and one couple leans in and whispers something while staring at us.

In a small town like this, people talk...and a strange woman flirting with Bobby Sweet is likely to cause quite a commotion.

I should probably be more concerned about it, but I just soak up the way his smile lights up his face and his eyes dance with amusement.

"Yeah. Bobby Bond." He creates a fake gun with this free hand and makes shooting motions toward me. "Pew. Pew. Taking down boring meals left and right to ensure the world is a safe place for fine cuisine."

It's cheesy as hell—and really, not even that funny —but I can't stop the laugh that bubbles up from my chest.

God, Ash, you sound like a schoolgirl giggling at her crush.

But it's impossible to resist him and his presence. Since the moment we met up this morning in the market to start our interview for the story, it's been the easiest and most laid-back one I've ever conducted. Almost like I'm talking with someone I've been friends with my entire life instead of a complete stranger.

A devilishly handsome stranger with an apparently large appendage and skilled hands...

All the things I *shouldn't* be thinking about right now.

I *should* concentrate on the story...on what makes him a great chef and why Sweet Home Kitchen is so loved by anyone who eats there.

Already, I can see why people go to his place. He's likely the type of chef who walks around and greets every table and regales them with stories about his family recipes and offers an award-winning smile. The same one that makes spring butterflies dance in my stomach like I'm some damn teenager, rather than a thirty-year-old, professional woman working on a story.

If I can't reel myself back in, this interview could go sideways quick, and the last thing I need is the paper getting wind of me doing something that could get me fired—like jumping the bones of Bobby Sweet instead of tasting his delectable dishes.

Space.

That's what I need—space.

I take a step to my right, putting a little more distance between us as we stroll through the rest of the market. Despite having moved away slightly, Bobby's free hand brushes against mine, sending a slight spark shooting up my arm.

What the hell was that?

That familiar warmth spreads through me, and I tuck my hair back behind my ear again to give me something to do with my hands in order to avoid any more inadvertent touching.

Or was it intentional?

I peek at Bobby out of the corner of my eye, but his focus remains in front of us or to the sides on the various stands. If it was intentional, he isn't giving me any indication of it as we make our way past the last stall and toward the restaurant, two blocks down along Main Street.

Peering down at the two small canvas bags hanging from his hand, I frown. "Are you sure you have everything we need?"

I'm no cooking expert—far from it—but they don't seem to hold enough ingredients to make anything, let alone a dish so good that it got him such incredible honors.

Foodie Magazine called it "a revelation" and "one of the most unique takes on the classic they had ever eaten."

Yet, the man only bought things from three stalls.

Either he is a true miracle worker, or I have been doing things all wrong in the kitchen all these years...when I'm actually *in* the kitchen—which is rarely.

He peeks at me out of the corner of his eye and offers a little crooked grin. "Oh, ye of little faith. I could go dumpster diving behind the supermarket and cook you a five-star, four-course meal. Here"—he holds up the bags and jostles them playfully—"we have the finest produce and meat the Midwest has to offer."

"I believe you." The vendors at the stands clearly care deeply about what they sell and only provide the highest quality local ingredients—potentially grown with dog shit. "It just doesn't seem like very much."

"Sometimes, the simplest dishes are the most delicious."

I pull out my small notepad and pen from my jacket pocket and quickly jot that down.

Bobby barks out a laugh that makes me jerk my head back up. "Did you just write that down?"

He leans over to the side to try to see the page, but I flip the notebook closed, the heat of embarrassment flooding my cheeks again, though I don't have the slightest clue why.

"Yeah..."

One of his dark eyebrows wings up at me. "Why?"

"Because I think it would make a great tagline for the article."

"Hmmm." He presses his lips together like he's pondering my statement. "Maybe, but I'm confident we can come up with something a little more interesting than that."

He winks at me, and it sends a brief flutter through my body.

God, why does that have to be so damn hot?

A guy winking should be *cheesy* and *lame*, not make me want to climb him like a damn tree and see if the rumors about *his* eggplant are true.

Keep it professional, Ashley.

Even if our playful banter is often bordering on flirtation, that's as far as it can go. I need to keep my job, and letting Bobby Sweet get to me will only lead down the road to unemployment.

Fucking the subject of your interview is generally frowned upon my mainstream media outlets...

Go figure.

We finally arrive outside Sweet Home Kitchen, and he unlocks the front door and holds it open for me —ever the small-town gentleman he appears to be.

Why can't he be a total asshole?

It would make this so much easier.

Stepping into the restaurant, a blanket of comfort and homey welcoming immediately settles over me. A sense of peace that makes me want to stay forever.

The rustic wood tables, white linen tablecloths, empty wine bottles with flowers as the centerpieces, all remind me of every down-home restaurant I ever went to growing up. Places that always had incredible food and stellar people working in them.

"This place is amazing." The mural on the far wall

depicts a sunset over crystal blue waters of what must be the Mediterranean—as beautiful as if I were looking at it in person. "Who did that amazing mural?"

Bobby stops to stand in front of it. "Believe it or not, my sous chef, Amanda."

"Really?"

He nods. "She's incredibly talented—both in art and cooking. She got both her culinary degree and went to art school before she started working here."

"Wow."

A grin pulls at his lips. "And I got free labor."

I narrow my eyes on him. "I don't know if you're joking or not."

"Of course, I'm joking. I paid her for her artwork."

"Good, I'd hate to write in my article that you're a total cheapskate."

His jaw drops incredulously. "A cheapskate? You just watched me spend over a hundred dollars to buy three eggplants, a handful of tomatoes, some potatoes, lamb, and some herbs."

"True, but you might have been buttering up the stall owners to ensure that you get the best pick of their produce each week."

He narrows his rich amber eyes on me. They dance with mischief as he examines me in silence for what feels like a full minute. "Someone's let you in on my secrets."

I raise my eyebrows at him. "Does that mean you have to kill me now?"

He barks out a laugh and pushes through the

swinging door to the kitchen. "Depends on what you're going to print in your article."

Definitely not *that his mother is a shitty cook...*

"Well, I haven't even finished the interview yet, so I can't make that determination at this point."

Though, I have no doubt what I end up taking to print will be complimentary of this man...and his food.

Keep it about the food, *Ash!*

A grin plays at his lips, and he sets the bags on the long metal counter and reaches for the hem of his T-shirt, pulling it up and over his head.

I quickly cover my eyes with my hand, but not before his rippling six pack and hard pecs are seared into my vision permanently. "What are you doing?"

His low chuckle makes my thighs clench and has my imagination running wild about how it would feel against my skin.

"Putting on my chef's coat."

"Why does that require taking off your shirt?"

And getting me all hot and bothered?

He laughs again, the light brush of fabric moving as he dresses mingling with the sound that does things to me that I don't even want to acknowledge. "You ever cooked in a restaurant kitchen before, Miss Wells?"

"No. I leave that to the professionals."

I'd much rather buy an amazing meal than try to cook it on my own and mess it up—which happens more often than I care to admit—especially to a man as talented as Bobby Sweet.

"Well, it gets very hot in here—very quickly."

I jerk away from his voice that's suddenly much closer than it was before. The man must be standing right in front of me now, within reach, if I simply lifted my free hand and brushed it against his hard body.

He snuck up on me—in more ways than one.

"You can lower your hand, Miss Wells." Amusement laces his every word. "I'm decent."

Reluctant to have to face him, I lower it and find him doing the last button on the chef's coat with a smirk.

He leans even closer, waggling his eyebrows again. "But if you liked what you saw, you can wait until I'm done cooking and see it again when I take this off."

My jaw drops before I can stop it, and another blush attacks my pale skin.

Forward much?

Though it didn't offend me.

Not in the least.

It sends a thousand distinct possibilities racing through my head. My fingers itch to touch that smooth expanse of hard flesh, but instead, I grab my pen and notepad to keep my hands busy and sit on the edge of the counter—well away from where Bobby will work to prepare the meal that brought me here.

He rifles through the fabric bags and removes all the ingredients he purchased at the market today— fresh basil, heirloom tomatoes, eggplant, potatoes, and ground lamb, along with a few other things. "No need to blush, Miss Wells. I understand we're just professional colleagues."

I clear my suddenly parched throat and glance around the kitchen to avoid his heated gaze or imaging him shirtless again. "Yes, exactly. Professional. I'm going to observe while you do your thing and take some notes. I may interject a question or two when I have it."

That panty-melting grin of his makes another appearance, and he winks. "Ask anything you want. I'm an open book."

There are so many things.

Do you have a girlfriend?

Am I imagining this?

Is this how you are with all women, or do you just want to ensure you get a good write up?

Why are men so damn *frustrating?*

But I don't dare ask them.

That would be unprofessional—which I am at least *trying* not to be, even when this man is making it increasingly difficult.

I watch the charming Bobby Sweet whip through the ingredients with his chef's knife, slicing and dicing and julienning so quickly I can barely keep up. His laser focus on what he's doing gives me an opportunity to examine him without feeling like a big creeper.

It's business—I *have* to watch his every single move and tattoo every detail of him into my mind for later— to write the story.

Definitely *not* to rub one out to.

His strong jaw line...

Beautiful Greek statute body and profile...

The way has big, powerful hands so deftly handle the knife...

God, I bet he's good with his hands.

So, so good.

My tongue darts out across my lips, but it has nothing to do with the food he's handling and everything to do with the chef preparing it.

He tosses ingredients into various pots and pans and skillets on the stove, glancing at me once in a while with a mischievous smirk, perhaps waiting for me to ask a question, but at this point, I'm just enjoying watching the show.

"You don't have anything to ask me?"

His question jerks me from my daze, and I shift on the hard metal beneath me as I try to regain my composure and not appear like I was caught ogling him.

"Oh, well..." I peek down at my notepad and the little scribbled heart with Bobby's name in the middle of it.

Oh, my God! When the hell did I do that?

Am I five again?

I clear my throat and flip to another page to ensure he doesn't see that embarrassment. "I think I'm good right now."

He smiles and raises an eyebrow. "You look a little...*thirsty*."

You have no idea...

I am *definitely* parched.

Another smirk tilts his lips. "Can I offer you a glass of wine?"

Not exactly what I'm thirsty for...

Not that I would tell *him* that. "Is wine really appropriate while we're doing an interview?"

His shoulders rise and fall nonchalantly in his still-pristine white chef's coat. "You tell me. I don't do a lot of interviews. But we're standing in my kitchen, and let me tell you what my grandmother and mother always told me—you don't cook without a glass of wine within reach."

Charming...

And maybe some liquid courage might release some of this awkward tension and let me finish my job without doing or saying something stupid. "You twisted my arm."

"Good." He grins and disappears into the restaurant, then returns with two red wine glasses and a bottle tucked under his arm. He sets down the glasses and turns the bottle toward me. "Xinomavro. Have you ever had it?"

"No, but I've heard they're incredible."

"They are, and often very difficult to come by around here, but I have a supplier in Chicago who sends me everything I need."

"You don't have to open anything special for me."

He pulls out a wine opener and removes the cork with a satisfying pop that makes me jump. "I have to disagree with that, Miss Wells. I think you deserve the best of everything imaginable, and once you taste what I have planned, you're going to understand what that really is."

Chapter Three

BOBBY

I step through the swinging door into the restaurant and grab two wine glasses and a bottle of Xinomavro, unable to fight the grin pulling at my lips.

The entire day, I've walked a very fine line between professional and shameless flirting with the sexy reporter—the latter being immensely more fun—and this bottle of wine may be just what she needs to finally loosen up a little and enjoy our time together in more than an interviewer/interviewee capacity.

I push back into the kitchen and round the counter to face her where she sits perched, her long, shapely legs on display in the cute white sundress that leaves little to the imagination. Every single luscious curve of her shapely body draws my eyes to it, and I finally have to force myself to look away in order to deal with the wine and not look like a perv staring.

The glasses clink against the metal as I set them

down, and I turn the bottle toward Ashley. "Xino-mavro. Have you ever had it?"

Her perfect pink bow lips twist as she examines the bottle. "No, but I've heard they're incredible."

"They are, and often very difficult to come by around here, but I have a supplier in Chicago who sends me everything I need."

She pulls back slightly, her hand pressed against her chest. "You don't have to open anything special for me."

I pull out a wine opener and remove the cork with a satisfying pop that makes Ashley jump. Barely managing to bite back my laugh at her adorable reaction, I shake my head. "I have to disagree, Miss Wells. I think you deserve the best of everything imaginable, and once you get a taste of what I have planned, you're going to understand what that *really* means."

My eyebrows waggle almost of their own accord, and Ashley's mouth hangs open momentarily, her long, thick black lashes blinking rapidly across large green eyes as she tries to conjure up a response.

Okay, maybe that was a little too forward.

But the moment I met her at the market for this interview, her beauty struck me like a runaway freight train. Her shiny blond hair, and her cute as hell button nose, pouty pink lips, and a body I'd love to take my slow, sweet time to learn my way around...all of it has been driving my cock wild all damn afternoon.

I should be more professional, dial back the banter a couple dozen notches, but every time my mouth opens, innuendos seem to tumble out, and I have zero ability to bite back the words.

How I'd love to actually partake in some of the things racing through my head.

"Excuse me?" The question comes in a deeper, almost sultry voice I haven't heard from her today.

It goes straight to my cock, which stirs in the confines of my pants, pressing painfully against the zipper.

Down boy.

Thank fuck my chef's coat provides a bit of coverage for my response to her, or this interview would take one hell of an awkward turn. As it stands, the banter and flirting have flown so naturally between us that it's felt comfortable and "right."

Shit. I hope I didn't just fuck that up.

I pick up her glass and begin pouring wine, pretending like my dick isn't growing rock hard right in front of her.

Nothing to see here.

Just a man pouring a glass of wine for a *professional* colleague to enjoy while the spicy moussaka finishes baking.

Though, it's not what has my mouth watering as I imagine eating it...

Shaking my head, I try my damnedest to get my mind off *my* needy, throbbing eggplant and on to the actual eggplant at hand. The real reason this stunning, fascinating woman is here—to interview me.

This is huge for Sweet Home Kitchen. Things have

been going so well since I came home, and especially since Mary came back to help run the catering side of the business. I don't need to blow this opportunity by being a horn-dog.

But damn, she makes it hard.

My cock jumps in response, pressing even more firmly against its zippered confines.

Yeah, she certainly is making it hard right now.

I hand her the glass of wine and try not to fantasize about her swallowing something else as she raises it to her lips and takes her first sip.

She moans, a tiny, almost needy little sound deep in her throat.

Fuck, that's sexy.

The eggplant in my pants seems to agree, twitching and throbbing to be let out to play.

She sets down the glass before running her tongue across her bottom lip to lap up a small droplet of wine that rests there. My eyes follow her every move while my dick tries its best to punch its way out of my pants.

And I can't focus for shit.

Thank fuck the moussaka is already in the oven.

With the distraction Ashley Wells is causing, I'd probably burn the bechamel if I were trying to do it now.

I reach down and open the door to check on the progress. The slightest hints of golden brown are *just* appearing on the top, which means we're close.

And I'm close to losing my will power.

All the thoughts and ideas stirring inside my head

right now mostly involve both of us in some various forms of nudity, but she doesn't need to know that...just yet.

It's clear she wants to remain professional while conducting this interview, so I'll do my best to keep it that way—as long as I can. Which means explaining my comment without sounding like a sex crazed dick.

Come on, Bobby, get your shit together.

"The moussaka I prepared...once you taste it, it'll knock your panties off."

"Socks." She clears her throat, shifting on the counter again as her brow furrows. "The saying is knock your *socks* off."

Shit! I said panties.

I can't seem to get my mind out of the gutter with this woman. If we had met under different circumstances, I might already have her spread out on my bed, devouring every fucking inch of her.

But that isn't in the cards right now.

"That's what I said." I cover by reaching for my glass and filling it up. Maybe I overfill it a bit because, honestly, I could really use a drink.

I set down the bottle of wine before I take a good, long pull from the glass. The slightly chilled liquid does nothing to quell the fire burning through my body just being near this voluptuous, brilliant woman. Neither does downing almost half the glass.

Ashley observes me and takes another small sip of her wine, then reaches for her pen and notepad again, returning herself to "professional" mode. "Are there any secret ingredients in this dish that make it special?"

The scent of the eggplant, lamb, tomato sauce and herbs permeates the air, and I suck in a deep breath of it that brings with it hundreds of beautiful memories.

"It's made with love." I smirk at her and take a sip of my wine.

She rolls her eyes and scoffs.

"I'm serious." I point my glass toward the stove. "My grandmother on my mom's side used to make this for me and my sister at least once a week. She came to live with us when we were very young, and she and my mother taught me everything that I know about cooking. The last time she made it was to celebrate my graduation from culinary school."

I release a little sigh and blink away the burn in my eyes.

"I can still see her so proudly setting that dish out on the table before her family. She filled everything with love—as cheesy as that may sound."

Ashley watches me, her eyes shimmering slightly with unshed tears.

Shit. It wasn't supposed to sound sad.

"That's a beautiful memory, Bobby."

That really brought the whole vibe down.

I lean closer to her so I can whisper conspiratorially. "Yes, it is. And if I told you what the *real* secret ingredient is, the thing that makes it extra spicy, I'd have to kill you."

She bursts out laughing, the sound tinkling and

light, filling the space between us, and I pull back with my own chuckle, thankful to have broken that emotional moment quickly.

Finishing my glass of wine, I set down the glass and pull open the oven to check the dish again. The perfect bubbly brown surface greets me, and I grin and grab the hot pads to remove it.

Ashley watches intently from her perch, which gives her the perfect perspective to watch all the prep I did and to see the ultimate creation. I tilt it toward her, and she releases a little *ooooo* sound that twitches my cock back to life.

Hell.

I grit my teeth and set the tray on the counter, then motion toward the chef's table set up in the kitchen's corner. "Take a seat while I plate this up."

She slides off the counter in a way I know she doesn't intend to be seductive, but it still sends a rush a heat through my body that has nothing to do with the piping hot spicy moussaka in front of me.

Grabbing the bottle of wine and our glasses, she glances at the tray before flashing me a grin. "Looks delicious."

You sure do...

The words *almost* slip out of my mouth, but I somehow manage to contain them long enough to cut out two pieces and plate them up exactly how we serve it in the restaurant.

My heart thunders against my ribcage as I approach the table and my waiting critic.

God, I hope she loves this.

And it isn't just about her article or the write-up she's going to give me. I *need* her to like it, to love what I can do, to appreciate it and me.

God, that sounds lame.

I slip the plate onto the table in front of her and take the seat directly across from her with my own.

She looks down at it, her mouth slightly open in awe. "This looks amazing." She closes her eyes and takes a deep inhale. "And it smells divine. I can't wait to taste this."

I can't wait to taste you...

Her focus shifts up from her plate to me, and her brow furrows slightly. "Everything okay?"

Shit.

I was staring at her for what must be the hundredth time since she showed up today. Gawking isn't usually my thing, but I can't stop myself from looking at her—that shiny blond hair, those full lush lips that I want to kiss...and do other things to. "Yes, everything is great."

"I guess I only have one last question for you, Chef."

I pour us each a fresh glass of wine and bring mine to my lips for another sip. "What's that?"

Please let it be, "Hey, Bobby, this eggplant looks great, but I'd rather have your eggplant instead. Is that okay with you?"

I practically choke on my wine, trying to contain my laughter at my thought.

What would little Miss Perky Tits over there think

if she knew all I could think about today was spreading her out on my table and feasting on her?

"You okay?" she asks around a mouth of moussaka. "This is amazing, by the way."

I diffuse the situation and my thoughts. "Thank you and excuse me, wine went down the wrong way." I thump my chest and fake a cough. "What was your question?"

"How does Chef Sweet change the face of modern dining?"

A laugh bubbles from my chest, and I offer her a genuine smile. Looking at her beautiful evergreen eyes, mesmerizing and shining under the restaurant lights, I honestly couldn't have planned for a better question.

I wink at her. "One plate at a time."

Ashley cocks her head to the left, assessing me before laughter peels from deep within her. "Oh, my gosh, Bobby. I don't know where you get this stuff from, but that was a good one!" She raises her glass to me in a toast. "To Bobby, the king of eggplants!"

"Here, here!" I cheer and clink her glass.

I have another eggplant for her.

One that puts Old Jerry's to shame and hasn't stopped straining against my jeans for a damn hour.

We eye each other over the rim of our glasses for a moment, then carry on eating in companionable silence.

The moussaka tastes as good as it did when Yaya made it for us—only slightly different with my secret ingredients—fresh cayenne and hot paprika. It's what gives the dish a special heat moussaka often lacks. The kind of heat we probably don't need added to the flames already sizzling between us.

Every few moments, Ashley releases a moan that pierces through the comfortable quiet like a knife and goes straight to my cock.

Everything she does is sexy, and I don't think she even realizes it. Not when her perfect lips wrap around her fork. Not when she closes her eyes and hums in delight at the flavors of the dish I prepared just for her.

"So good." She sets down her cutlery and leans back in her chair. "I am stuffed."

And I can't take this sexual tension any fucking longer.

"Did you get everything you needed for the story?" I slide my plate out of the way and take one last drink of my wine.

She bobs her head and smiles. "Yeah, I believe that's it for our interview. I think I have everything I need. Thank you again, Chef Bobby."

The way she almost purrs my name is like fuel on the fire of my already burning libido.

"Good." I grin at her. "Miss Wells, are you ready for dessert?"

She pats her stomach as she exhales. "I'm not sure that I could eat another bite."

"I didn't ask you if you wanted to *eat* dessert." I push back my chair and walk around the table, hoping like hell that I'm not getting the wrong idea about what's been happening all day.

I'm fucking going for it.

"Bobby, I..." She brushes her blond locks out of her face, her lips twisting in confusion. "I don't understand."

"Don't you?" I raise a brow at her. "Am I the only one feeling this thing between us?"

I lock eyes with her, willing her to want this moment—no, *need* this moment as much as I do.

All of this flirty, sexy banter has been driving me insane.

I grab the arms of her chair, turning it toward me slightly, caging her in. The position brings me close enough for the delectable scent that's all Ashley to waft over me. My entire body tenses, and I take a deep inhale, even knowing what it will do to me. I want a fucking taste of her so badly I might fucking explode in my pants before I can even see if she is on board with this madness.

Though we just met, our chemistry is undeniable. I've already thrown caution to the wind at this point. I can only hope like hell she's on the same page as me.

Fuck it.

She stares up at me, her green eyes wide, her mouth open slightly. Soft, warm pants of breath slip from between her lips.

I run a hand down her cheek, and she leans into my touch.

Fuck yes.

Dropping my head even closer, I brush my lips against her ear. "What if you're my dessert?"

Chapter Four

BOBBY

I pull back to examine her, and it takes a second for my words to register before her eyes widen slightly and she gifts me with one of her gorgeous smiles that curve her sinfully perfect lips.

God, she is stunning.

Her hand slides up over mine on her cheek, and she squeezes it gently, almost in invitation. "What did you have in mind, Chef?"

"The better question is...what *don't* I have in mind?"

A million images of her, naked in every position imaginable, race through my head. I don't think we have enough time to do everything I want to. She pulls my hand away and presses a kiss to my palm. Chills skate along my flesh from only a simple brush of her lips.

I've got it fucking bad for her...

Ashley is the sexiest woman I have ever seen in my

entire life, and I plan to thoroughly enjoy every single inch of her.

"Mmm..." Her soft hum of appreciation vibrates through my palm. "I like the sound of that, Chef. And now that the interview is done, how about you just show me?"

Sweet mother of God!

She reaches out, grips my jacket, and yanks, pulling my mouth to hers. I close my eyes, moaning at the first taste of her crossing my lips and grip the back of her head, holding her in place for a kiss that makes the entire world around us disappear. Nothing matters right now except the press of her mouth against mine.

Every swipe of her tongue. Every little mewl she makes. The way her fingers dig into my jacket, clinging to me like a damn lifeline. It's all too much.

I pry my mouth off hers. "Hold on."

Confused green eyes meet mine, and I grip her waist and lift her from her chair. She squeaks and wraps her arms around my neck as I turn and set her onto the top of the table.

"What, what are you doing?" she manages to ask in between frantic kisses.

My God, have I ever felt lips this soft before?

I grip her flats in my hands and slip them both off at the same time, letting them drop to the floor without a care where they land.

"This little sundress has been killing me all day."

When she showed up at the market in this, I could barely contain myself. Even though it's casual and flowy and completely professional, especially with the jean jacket she wore over it initially, all I could think about was what was underneath it.

Ashley smiles at me, batting her eyelashes playfully. "Really? This old thing?"

She lifts her hips, and I pull it up and over her head, letting it join her shoes on the floor.

Hell.

I almost come on the spot as I let my eyes wander over her spread out on *my* chef's table in her matching pale blue lace bra and panty set.

"Fuck."

She wraps her legs around my waist and pulls me close. "That's the plan, Chef."

Apparently, I read this situation all *sorts* of right.

Thank fuck for that.

Ashley makes quick work of getting off my chef's jacket in between heated kisses, and by the time it joins the growing pile of clothing on the tile, I'm so worked up that it's only through sheer will that I haven't already blown my load in my pants.

"You're the most beautiful woman I've ever seen."

I pepper kisses across her cheek and work my way down her neck and across her full breasts, savoring the warm flavor of her delicate skin. Her pebbled nipple strains against the pale lace, and I bite at the pale flesh, relishing the little yelp of surprise and moan of pleasure she releases in response.

There's nothing sexier than a woman knowing what she wants and being vocal when she gets it, and

Ashley appears to be that and then some. Any reservations about acting on our clear connection seem to have disappeared the moment she completed the interview.

And it couldn't have come a second too soon.

I slide my hands around her waist, grasp both sides of her panties, and tug them down her shapely legs. Ashley lifts her hips up off the table one at a time so I can slide the thong free. Once I pull it off, I tuck her panties into my pocket with a smug grin.

"Hey! That's my thong!"

She laughs, trying to reach for them, but I playfully bat her hands away, blocking all her attempts to retrieve the lacey garment.

I chuckle under my breath. "They're mine now." I lean over her and brush my lips across her. "*And so are you.*"

There are so many damn things I want to do to this woman, but scanning around us, the honey syrup from making baklava earlier today gives me an incredible new one.

My mouth waters, and I twine my hands in her hair and kiss Ashley so intensely, so thoroughly, that by the time we come up for air, I'm dizzy with lust and desire.

This is all unfamiliar territory for me.

It feels like I'm on the highest peak, looking out at the world of possibilities that lay before me.

"I'm ready for dessert. Be a good girl and lie back on the table for me, Ash."

A giggle slips from her kiss-swollen lips, and she does as instructed. "Oh, shit. Oh. Okay."

Once she's spread out on the table before me, I can't help but to pause, taking in every stunning, glorious inch of her—a feast fit for a king. A woman who could so easily be my queen.

"Ashley..." I breathe her name like the most sacred prayer. "You are magnificent."

I pull the syrup off the counter and dip my finger in it, watching her eyes grow wide. Grinning, I hold up my finger to her mouth for her to taste. "I'm a chef, Ash. You didn't think I might want to play with some food?"

She latches onto my finger, sucking it into her mouth, her tongue swirling every last bit of the sticky syrup from it. Every swipe goes straight to my cock as if she were licking and sucking it instead of my finger.

If I don't fuck this woman soon, the foreplay may kill me.

With a contented moan and a pop, she releases my finger and her tongue darts out across her lips.

I groan and lean over to kiss her briefly, her mouth tasting of honey, cayenne, and a flavor that is all Ashley.

It's a heady combination—one I wish I could hold in my mouth forever the way I'm locking this memory into my brain.

But there's something I need to do more than kiss her.

I pull my lips free from hers, and she tugs at my

hair, trying to pull me back to her—to no avail. I'm a man on a mission. And I won't stop until it's complete.

Kissing my way down her neck toward her breasts, I tug the cups of her bra down and lavish each beaded tip with attention. Licking, nipping, and sucking before kissing my way down her stomach.

"Oh, Jesus..." Her moan fills the kitchen, and she throws her arm over her eyes, her body tensing in anticipation.

"No, sweetheart. It's Bobby." I blow on her mound and delight as goosebumps break out across her flawless skin. "Move your arm and watch me eat you."

"Oh, hell..." she murmurs, but she drops her arm.

Those expressive eyes lock onto mine, and I inhale her sweet fragrance briefly before I drag the chair from behind me and take a seat between her spread thighs.

I lean forward but stop short of my mouth hitting her bare pussy.

Inhaling again, I can't bite back my response as my cock aches. "*Fuck*. I can't wait to see how you taste."

Her body shifts across the wood in anticipation of what's coming, and I spread her sweet cunt apart with my fingers and groan.

Fuck, is she wet.

"You're wet for me, Ash."

Not a question. A goddamn fact.

Ashley is just as worked up as I am, and that is a damn turn on.

I lick her in one long swirl from bottom to top, stopping to toy with her clit. That little sensitive bundle of nerves begs for attention, and I blow on it then lick. Blow, then lick. Building her up for what I have planned.

"Mmm." She purrs like a damn kitten and bites her lip, arching her hips toward me, begging for more contact.

Sucking her clit between my lips, I dip my finger back into the syrup. Her eyes trace my every move, and she watches me pull back slightly and spread it across her most sensitive spot.

She is definitely the tastiest dessert I've ever had, and I need more.

So much more.

I've never been so fucking hungry in my entire life.

I lean in, licking the syrup from her body as I slide two fingers into her wet pussy. Her fingers tangle in my hair, and she holds me firm, riding my face while I fuck her with my hand and suck mercilessly on her clit.

She can barely keep her eyes open. Her hooded gaze watches me while her body shifts and contorts. "Bobby, I'm going to come."

Fuck yeah, you are!

Her moaned warning only drives me to go harder, to suck faster, to demand more from her. And a few seconds later, I'm rewarded with her orgasm slamming into her prone body.

She thrashes against the table, clinging to my head and bucking her hips, driving them against my face in desperation until she gasps and turns boneless.

But I'm not finished yet.

Far from it.

I kiss each of her thighs as I spread her legs a little wider, making room for my next idea.

Her eyes flutter open, and Ashley watches me from beneath hooded lids as I reach for the large purple ingredient that brought us together today in the first place.

Mild panic widens her gaze. "Bobby, um, there's no *way* that will fit in there."

I bark out a laugh and drag it across her thighs, then lightly trace it back and forth over her sensitive clit.

She has no idea what her body is capable of...

And I'm going to show her.

I work her up, alternating between lapping at her clit and teasing her entrance with the eggplant. It's the kinkiest thing I've ever done in my life, and my cock is weeping to get inside of her.

It's time for her to see what I have for her and find out what she's willing to take.

I push up to my feet and jiggle the eggplant in front of her. "You think this won't fit?"

Her lust-soaked gaze zeroes in on the mammoth aubergine, and she braces herself on her elbow shakes her head. "No, no way."

Grinning, I set it on the table beside her and quickly undo my button and zipper so I can slide my jeans down. Her focus dips to my cock, and she inhales deeply as I take it in my hand and give it a hard stroke.

"What about this?" I lean over her and brush the

44

head of my dick through her wet pussy lips. "Do you think you can take this?"

"Holy hell, Bobby. I thought you were joking about the eggplant." She sucks in another little breath, her lips mere centimeters from mine. "You're fucking huge."

I kiss her gently, letting my tongue twine with hers as I brush my cock through her release and against her clit, over and over, making her squirm beneath me. "I am, baby. But I know you can take it. You can take me."

She gasps and arches against me, allowing me to nudge the head just inside her wet heat. *"Fucking hell, Bobby...I sure hope so."*

Chapter Five

ASHLEY

Bobby nudges the head of his cock a fraction of an inch deeper into me. My pussy clenches around it, reluctant to take such a large invasion. His jaw locks. A muscle there tics, and he tightens his grip on my hair.

"Relax, Ash..." He nips at my lips. "You can take it. You can take me."

I release a heavy breath, trying to let me body relax.

He eases in slowly, his mammoth length and girth stretching me open.

"Oh, God..." My eyes drift closed and my body tenses against the intrusion, wanting it and not entirely sure I can take all of it at the same time.

"Shhh." He brushes his lips over mine again. "Relax, Ash. I won't hurt you."

He won't.

I *know* he won't.

But he's so damn *big*.

He puts Old Jerry's eggplant we were joking about at the market to shame.

And here I thought we were just joking around.

Men always love to brag about the size of their... appendage. And none of them have ever measured up, in my experience.

Pipe dreams of men with tiny dicks.

This isn't a dream though; this is *very, very real*.

"Ash, look at me." His low, gritty voice draws my eyes open to meet his amber ones. "Relax, breathe."

I suck in a deep breath and force my body to relax. Concentrate on the hot press of his body, his large hands gripping me, his lips moving against mine.

He pushes inside slowly, deeper and deeper, until he's finally seated fully inside me.

Hell...

"Fuck, Ash..." He drags his head back, and his jaw tightens again. "You feel fucking incredible."

All I can manage in response is a little gasping sound, and he captures my mouth with his and draws his hips back slowly. The long drag of the ridge of the head of his cock against my G-spot makes my entire body spasm and my pussy clasp around him again.

He groans and drives back into me, faster this time, harder, my body welcoming all of him, all the initial tension and worry melting away with the ecstasy burning through my veins like a wildfire.

The entire day has been a slow build to this. It was

inevitable, really. Fighting it to try to remain professional may have been necessary, but so is this.

It's why I finally gave in to what I wanted. To what I've been feeling since the moment we met. This feels right. Exactly where I should be and exactly who I should be with.

Bobby Sweet is a master in the kitchen, and apparently, in the bedroom.

Or on the table...as it might be.

Every fiber of my being vibrates with the need for him to keep going. Each thrust of his hips pushes me closer toward another release my body so badly needs. His lips pressed to mine, his hot breath, and the tiny sounds of pleasure he makes...

How did I live without this before?

How did I live without Bobby Sweet?

His cock driving into me while his tongue tangles with mine is the type of perfection I never knew existed. A feeling of being full, content, *whole* for the first time in my entire life.

All because this man knows how to handle an eggplant.

And God...does he EVER!

My belly full of the delicious meal and my pussy full of his enormous cock equal absolute contentment. And the deep rumble of his satisfied groan vibrating from his chest to mine assures me he's on the same page.

"Christ, Ash, you're fucking perfect."

His large hands slide down my body to find my

hips. He squeezes the flesh there, hard enough for it to hurt in a way that confirms he's barely holding on by a thread.

So am I.

It's so close, I can almost taste it, along with the heat and flavors of the dish he made me still lingering on my tongue. But there's something else I want to taste, too. My mouth waters for it, but I can't find my breath long enough to tell him how badly I want him to come down my throat.

He slides a hand across my mound and swirls his thumb over my clit, I collapse back onto the table and detonate. The orgasm slams into me so hard, my hips leap off the table, and he drives into me even deeper. So deep, it's like he's reaching my soul.

I thrash on him as he continues to thrust, his hand tightening on my hip, the muscles of his neck strained. My nails dig into the skin of his forearms, but he doesn't seem to mind.

As the sparks jolting through my body finally start to wane, and I roll my hips to meet his, clenching around him to finally draw out his release. He groans and locks his lust-soaked gaze with mine, then comes on a roar that reverberates off all the tile and metal in the kitchen and goes straight to my heart.

His body jerks a few times, then he collapses on top of me on the table, catching himself on his forearms to keep from completely crushing me. He lowers his mouth to mine and kisses me slowly, gently, almost reverently, then he rests his forehead to mine and lets out a long sigh.

I know the feeling...

The silence is comfortable, yet I want to say something. I want to mark this incredible occasion with some beautiful words to match it, but I can't manage to speak.

My entire body feels boneless and content, his cock still buried in me. I squeeze around him, and he groans and lifts his head again.

"You keep doing that, and we're going to have to go for round two before we even recover from round one."

I grin at him. "I have something else in mind."

One of his dark eyebrows rises slowly. "Oh, yeah? What's that? Because fucking you again sounds pretty incredible."

It does.

It really, really, really, really does.

I push myself up on my elbows and press my mouth to his, clenching around him so his groan slips between his lips and into mine. "I want you to come in my mouth this time."

He jerks his head back, his eyes narrowing on me. One of his hands reaches for my face, and he drags his thumb across my lips. "How did you get so fucking perfect?"

A laugh bubbles out and I shake my head. "I'm far from it. Give it some time and you'll see."

He grins at me. "Does that mean you want to spend more time with me?"

Oh, hell...

I hadn't even considered what was going to happen after I leave and drive back home tonight. Somehow, I became so wrapped up in the moment that I didn't think about what this might mean, if anything, to either of us.

Aside from a magnificent romp in the kitchen.

An ache forms in the center of my chest, and I swallow back a little cry of despair. "Um, I'd love to, but I live in Milwaukee, and you live here in Small-townsville."

His lips twist, and he brushes the hair back from my face and tucks it behind my ear. "You know, we have a pretty good local newspaper here in town that is always looking for excellent reporters. They haven't had anyone who could write worth a shit for years, though."

"What?" I shake my head, trying to clear the post-orgasmic haze to make sure I'm understanding him. "Are you saying I should move here?"

He can't mean that.

Another grin plays at his lips, but his eyes hold a dark concern. "That's exactly what I'm saying...*shit.*" He scrubs a hand over his face. "Did I just scare you away? This is too forward and too fast. I'm sorry. I—"

"Stop." I press my finger over his lips to halt his babbling. "I-I'm not sure how I feel."

He opens his mouth again to speak, but I press my finger there even harder.

"Just let me think. You just asked me to quit my job

and move here to be with you, but we've known each other for all of six hours."

His large hand wraps around my wrist, and he pulls my hand down, away from his mouth. "I know it sounds crazy. Believe me. I feel like maybe I'm losing my mind right now, but I don't want you to leave. The thought of you getting in your car and driving away tonight makes me want to smash everything in sight. Whatever happened between us today in those six hours is something way more than I've ever thought possible. I want you...no...*need* you to stay."

Holy hell, was that romantic.

And TERRIFYING.

I rub my hands over my face and try to make sense of the whirlwind this day has been.

He's right, though.

Whatever happened today doesn't just *happen*. It's a once in a lifetime thing. A kind of connection you don't get with just anyone.

Can I really walk away from it?

"I feel the same way, Bobby. But it's a huge step..."

He nods and takes my face between his palms to press a soft kiss against my lips. "It is. Huge. Life-changing. But so is what we just did." He shakes his head. "I don't do...*this*, with just anyone. It's been a long time for me, and I feel like there's a reason you ended up here today. At least give it a chance."

"A chance..."

A chance at what?

When the flirting led to...this, I assumed it was just going to be a spicy spring fling.

Can it really be more?

If I move here, it will give us a chance to find out, but if I get in my car and drive back home, we'll be hours away from each other, and that spells doom for any budding relationship.

Holy shit.

Relationship?

This was just *sex*.

Hot. Hot. *HOT* sex.

That's it, right?

Staring up at the sincerity in his gaze, that isn't so clear anymore.

He really means it.

He wants to *try*.

Jesus...I can't believe I'm going to say this.

I stare into his deep amber eyes and nod. "Okay."

His eyebrows fly up. "You'll stay?"

"I'll stay." I sigh and shake my head slightly. "Of course, I have to go back and try to figure out moving and the job thing, but I don't want to miss a chance to have whatever this is."

"But you'll stay tonight at least, right? You'll go back tomorrow?" He kisses me again, this time swirling his tongue against mine in a way that makes me clench around his cock again. "I need more time with you. I need it all."

Me, too.

"First, I need *your* eggplant in my mouth." I grin at him. "The rest, we can figure out later."

We hope you enjoyed this spicy bite!

More Smalltownsville food shenanigans are coming September 2023 with *Filthy Fall Flirt* !
Preorder now: books2read.com/FilthyFallFlirt

For another steamy story from Gwyn and Christy, check out *Royally Complicated*, our full-length super spicy bad boy royal/good girl commoner romance: books2read.com/RoyallyComplicated

To stay up to date on releases from Gwyn and Christy, sign up for Gwyn's newsletter here: www.gwynmcnamee.com/newsletter

ABOUT THE AUTHORS

Gwyn McNamee is an attorney, writer, wife, and mother (to one human baby and one fur baby). Originally from the Midwest, Gwyn relocated to her husband's home town of Las Vegas in 2015 and is enjoying her respite from the cold and snow. Gwyn loves to write stories with a bit of suspense and action mingled with romance and heat. When she isn't either writing or voraciously devouring any books she can get her hands on, Gwyn is busy adding to her tattoo collection, golfing, and stirring up trouble with her perfect mix of sweetness and sarcasm (usually while wearing heels). Gwyn loves to hear from her readers, and here's where you can find her:

Newsletter: www.gwynmcnamee.com/newsletter
Website: http://www.gwynmcnamee.com/
FB Reader Group: bit.ly/GwynMcNameeRG
Facebook: bit.ly/GwynMcNameeFB
Tiktok: bit.ly/TikTokGM

Instagram: bit.ly/GwynMcNameeIG
Twitter: bit.ly/GwynMcNameeTwitter
Goodreads: bit.ly/GwynMcNameeGR
Bookbub: bit.ly/GwynMcNameeBB

Writing with a whole lot of sarcasm and humor, mixed with a bit of Southern charm, Christy Anderson ain't no sweet tea kinda storyteller. As an author of romance, Christy believes it doesn't always have to be hearts and flowers; sometimes, it is dark and twisted, but romance nonetheless. She mixes terror, revenge, and a sliver of love and hope into stories about family, friends, struggles, blurred lines, and happily-ever-afters. Christy lives in the beautiful mountains of Eastern Tennessee with her husband and 152 cats (not really, but close), where she enjoys writing one twist at a time. Christy loves to hear from her readers, and here's where you can find her:

Newsletter: https://www.christyanderson.net/newsletter
Website: https://www.christyanderson.net/
Christy's Little Birds: bit.ly/ChristysReaderGroup
Facebook: bit.ly/ChristyAndersonFB
Instagram: bit.ly/ChristyAndersonInstagram
Goodreads: bit.ly/ChristyAndersonGoodreads
BookBub: bit.ly/ChristyAndersonBookBub

Made in the USA
Columbia, SC
23 September 2024

42209492R00035